Prologue
(that's the bit before the story)

You find yourself at a tournament. Knights armed with lances and atop horses run at each other as fast as they can. They try to knock one another off balance. Flags **wave** in the background. Trumpets da-da-da-**daaa**. Fans cheer and jeer. They munch on…on…whatever snack was popular in olden times. Maybe pop-beak. It's like popcorn. But, instead of corn kernels, it's pigeon beaks.

YUCK.

That sounds disgusting.

Good thing we just made it up.

Anyways, get ready to munch and crunch and **CHEER**—a medieval adventure awaits!

The Mustachioed Monster is the most feared knight
in all the land. Rumor has it that he dyes his famous
dark moustache with the blood of his opponents.

This, on the other hand, is ... well, *not* the most feared knight in all the land. Let's tune in to see if he can break his losing streak.

Who will win this epic fight? Why is that girl crying, **"STOP"?** Are those knights going to split one another in two? Is pop-beak actually a delicious snack?!

Want answers to those questions? Want to go on an adventure and actually find and experience those things?

You can! And you're about to!

But, for this adventure to end all adventures—to blow them **out of the water**—you'll need some background information.

We know, we know. You'll say, "C'mon! Get back to the adventure already!" And we *will* get back to the adventure already. But to make this adventure fan-**tas**-tic, you'll need some information to begin.

Psst, you—yes, you!—pay attention to the purple words.

So, without further ado:

Backstory

This is **Perri Petunia III**—those lines mean "the third." She is twelve years old. She insists on saying twelve and three-quarters. She likes reading. But she only says that to adults because they like to hear things like that. She prefers going on adventures with her brother, Archer. And playing softball.

This is **Archer.** He is nine. He's crazy about danger and adventure. He likes going on adventures to find his favorite things: pizza, goofy objects, and maps. He hates adventures that lead him to his least favorite things: vegetables, vegetables, and vegetables. He lettuce know that he really hates vegetables.

Yep, more backstory (sigh)

A lifetime ago, when she was seven years old, Eliza Effervescent—Aunt Bubbles to Perri and Archer—found a black silky hat that looked like a chimney pot. It kindled her love of collecting. Her wacky world of wonders began as a modest shack of shocking souvenirs. Then it morphed into a maze of mysteries until, finally, its size challenged the finest hotels in the world. It needed a new name—**"Lost & Found: The Effervescent Emporium of Curiosities."**

←— This is Aunt Bubbles, donning her Teasmaid Hat*

*patent pending

Even more backstory?! When will it end?!

Short story long: One of the most special, fantastic, un-be-*lieve*-able treasures arrived only two years ago. The story begins as most great stories do: It was a dark and stormy night. A woman hooked and crooked like a question mark entered Lost & Found. She opened a velvet box and bestowed a magical gift on Perri and Archer—a set of books that allowed them to travel through time. She said, "The pages of *The World Book* will *flutter*. The old grandmother clock will

BRONG and BRONG.

Delicate bubbles will ooze from the clock's face. Lost & Found will fade away, and your adventure will begin."

Short story shorter: A bent woman gave two kids a time-traveling device.

Chapter I: Thank goodness the backstory is over

Earlier today...

A paper ball hit Archer in the face.

"Oh, *it is on, Perri*," Archer **hissed.**

"I'm going to catch you!" Perri warned.

Archer accepted the challenge.

Perri darted behind a Grecian urn...over and under taxidermy animals...through a curly, swirly frame—all the while pelting Archer with wads of paper.

To dodge his sister's **powerful** shots—she was a softball player after all—Archer tried to blend in with various antiques throughout Lost & Found: The Effervescent Emporium of Curiosities.

   In the Grand Hall of Grandfather Clocks, Archer stood as straight as a board and

ticked

and

tocked.

And

ticked

and

tocked.

"Where are you, Archer? I promise I'll stop throwing paper."

In the Curious Cavern of Costumes, Archer cloaked himself in chain mail, a flexible armor made of small metal rings linked together. He s l o w e d his breathing…closed his eyes…and lifted a shield.

"Ha! Bullseye."

Plop.

The paper trickled to the ground.

"Ugh. So close. Hey…what's that design on the shield? Why is there a dragon?" Perri asked.

"I don't know … maybe something Aunt Bubbles added when she bought it? It sure makes it look cool," Archer said.

"I think it's a coat of arms, like what knights used in old times."

"Ahhh!" Archer screamed. "I don't want to hold something that used to be a coat made of-of-of arms!" He struggled to get his sentence out—the idea seemed so bizarre.

"No, silly. Not that kind of coat of arms. It has to do with symbols and heraldry. It's from medieval times," Perri replied.

"Medi-**EVIL?!?**" Archer exclaimed. "It certainly sounds **EVIL!**"

"I think it's time we look in *The World Book*," Perri concluded. "C'mon."

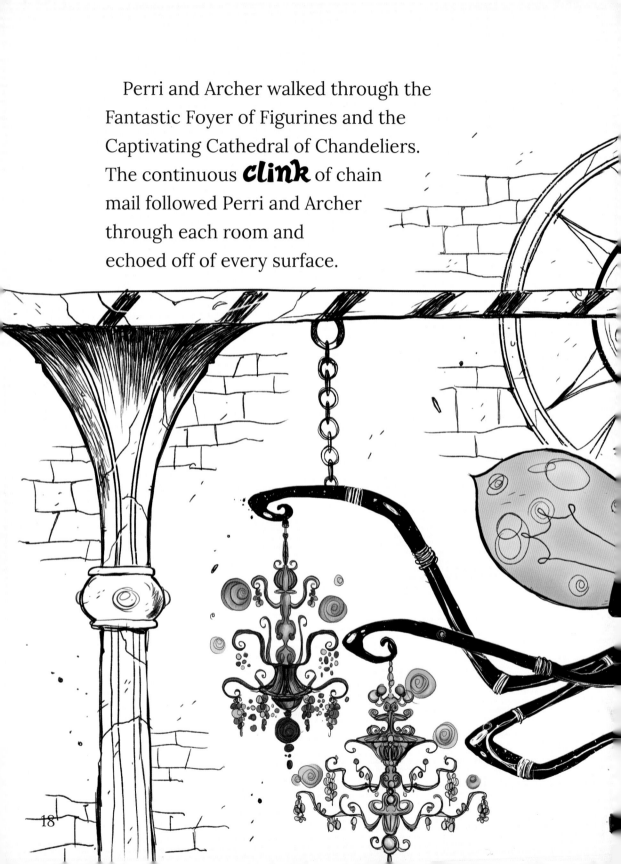

Perri and Archer walked through the Fantastic Foyer of Figurines and the Captivating Cathedral of Chandeliers. The continuous **clink** of chain mail followed Perri and Archer through each room and echoed off of every surface.

They rolled the shield like a wheel. It made a low rumble until they came to a stop at the worn library cart which housed their trusted guide: *The World Book.*

Perri s l o w l y dragged her fingers across each volume, coming to a rest on "H." A blur of pages later, they found images of coats of arms within the "Heraldry" article.

"See," Perri said. "Here it says, 'Heraldry is the study of a system of symbols used to represent individuals, families, countries, and such institutions as churches and universities.'"

Archer continued reading. "'The basic heraldic symbol is an emblem called a coat of arms, often known simply as arms.' So, like a flag?" Archer asked.

"I guess so," Perri said.

Archer took another volume off the shelf. "It says that 'medieval period' is from the Latin words medium (middle) and aevum (age). So it's not called medieval because it was **EVIL.** Phew!"

Perri continued reading. "It is 'a term that describes the period in European history from about the 400's through the 1400's.' Wow, I think that's way, way, *way* back when Aunt Bubbles was born."

"Yeah. I'm pretty sure her sixteenth birthday was, like, July 25th, 1210," Archer guessed. "Why is it called the 'Middle Ages'? Was it the middle child?"

"It says here that it was used because there was a gap between arts, culture, and society in the ancient world and that stuff in the 1300's and 1400's."

"So I guess the people who came up with the name in the 1300's thought they were in a time with a lot of art and culture?" Archer asked.

"I think—" but Perri couldn't finish her sentence.

BRONG

"Perri—look!" Archer pointed to the grandmother clock that towered over the kids. It was hooked and crooked like a question mark. The clock was so wonky that it looked like the face was upside down. The numbers and hands made a **mischievous** mask.

BRONG

"This can only mean one thing, Arch," Perri said, eyeing Archer and grinning a smile as wide as the grandmother clock was loud.

"Ready, Perri? But we can't—

BRONG

"—be traveling through time yet. There aren't any bubbles," Archer said, interrupted by the **BRONG, BRONG, BRONG** of the **BRONG-IEST** clock in all the land. Or at least in all of Lost & Found.

Delicate bubbles oozed from the grandmother clock. It was as if they were floating on itsy-bitsy bubbles, too.

Fragile. Graceful.

The **BRONG** of the grandmother clock was deafening. It wrapped Lost & Found in **BRONGS.** Perri thought that the bubbles made the sound a harp makes. Like the sound Aunt Bubbles made when she yawned.

The World Book grew lighter and lighter, like the light-as-a-bubble bubbles. The book opened and closed. Opened and closed. And, although the book was as old as Aunt Bubbles—maybe *even* older—the book fluttered with the speed of a hummingbird's wings.

Flip flip flip
Flip flip flip

"Here we go!" Archer **SHRIEKED** in delight.

Perri and Archer floated through time! Days and seconds. Years and months.

They somersaulted and cartwheeled past centuries and decades.

𝕮𝖍𝖆𝖕𝖙𝖊𝖗 II: The kids are dizzy. How 'bout you?

The kids landed with a **thud.**

Before they opened their eyes, they felt grass
tickling their necks.

"I don't think we are in Lost & Found anymore,
Archer," Perri said. "I wonder where we are this time."

"And when," Archer added, as he rolled off of the shield and pulled himself up on his elbows, extracting long blades of grass from his chain mail.

"Mmmm, I smell meat," Perri said.

"And freshly baked bread," Archer added.

"And honey!"

"And—yuck! *Dung*!" Archer shrieked.

Quickly helping one another up to avoid wallowing in dung, Archer and Perri began properly surveying their new surroundings. They rested on the shield. "A shield makes an excellent counter-on-the-go," Archer thought.

They could hear horns in the distance and saw smoke wafting into the sky. They were surrounded by massive horses covered in colorful fabrics and chain mail—much like the kind Archer was wearing. Striped tents and decorated banners made up the perimeter.

Perri and Archer turned in circles to take in their new environment—their new adventure.

"I see cliffs in the distance," Archer said.

Perri could see that his wheels were turning.

"What does that mean, Arch?" Perri asked.

"Well, cliffs and this type of ground—low mountains and hills—look a lot like England," Archer guessed. In truth, a lot of places in the world had cliffs, low mountains, and hills. So Archer wasn't totally sure. But he threw out an answer and said it confidently.

"I'm so glad you have your map and geography knowledge. You always know where we are in the world," Perri thanked her brother.

Suddenly, Archer was **whisked** away. He was ushered into line!

"Archer!" Perri yelled.

"Perri! Wh-wh-what do I do?" Archer yelled back. "Where am I going?!"

"Hail, fellow. Name and sport?" an old man asked. He looked down at Archer. "What? You are a child—a simple page! Is Sir Henry your knight, perchance?"

"Perchance?" Archer thought, "What does that mean?"

"Sir Henry is hither! See, he is summoning you!" the old man told Archer.

A man in shining armor was, in fact, summoning him. The knight—with armor so shiny you could use it as a mirror and red hair so bright that Archer questioned whether hair dye was around in … whatever time this was—intrigued Archer.

"Why yes—yes, I am his page!" Archer exclaimed. Then he remembered the shield in his hand. "See? I have his shield." This position of "page" sounded very important. Archer was hungry to do the duties of a page, whatever they might be.

"Run along, boy. Archery will begin anon," the old man said. "Good morrow, page. Next! Name and sport?" the old man asked the next person in line.

Archer weaved through the competitors to make his way to Sir Henry. He did not move as quickly as he would like, though, given that he was carrying a shield that was larger than he was. Despite the extra weight, Archer was nearly **vibrating** with excitement. His first job! He assumed his first job would be mowing lawns or scooping ice cream, not assisting a famous knight.

The knights's hot, metal armor felt good against his skin, even if he was bopping and banging into them. And—oh! An arrow pricked him in the eye!

Archer let out a **Squeal** that rivaled that of the pigs fearing their feasting fate. Fortunately, it was the nock—the blunt part of an arrow—and not the point. Aunt Bubbles would definitely know they'd been up to trouble if he returned without one eye.

Archer **scolded** himself for not traveling with his shield up. That's what it was for, wasn't it?!

With one eye covered, Archer searched for Perri. After struggling to lift the shield above his head until he finally succeeded, he determined that a shield also made an excellent sun visor.

He traveled especially slowly with one eye, an impossibly **HEAVY** shield, and chain mail that weighed—without him exaggerating and being absolutely accurate in his prediction—one million pounds.

"Hear ye! Hear ye! Archery will now take place. Sir Drake, Sir Paul …" the announcer declared, continuing to say other names, but Archer was busy trying to map out his new place of work—his office.

"Sir Henry, Sir Peter …" the announcer declared.

"Sir Henry! That's my boss," Archer thought, "I must find him." Archer made his way to the archery range, all the while **CHUCKLING** about how similar his name was to the sport.

He took this opportunity to search for Perri.

"Perri! Perri?" Archer cried.

He used his one good eye to spot her.

He saw rough, strong horses and silky, flowing
flags. He saw sturdy, stone walls and light, airy hay.
He saw rich, fatty mutton and honey-colored—Perri!

"Perri!" Archer cried.

"Archer! Where have you been? I have been looking everywhere for you!" Perri yelled.

Reunited, Perri and Archer hugged each other.

"What happened to your eye?" Perri asked.

"Oh, nothing. It's just a flesh wound. Perri, do you know where we are?" Archer asked.

"Well," Perri started, "you thought we were in England. And from the horses, knights, and castles, it seems like we are in medieval times. What do you think?"

"I think medieval might mean **EVIL** after all...," Archer said, thinking about his **THROBBING** eye.

Perri continued: "I think we are at a tournament. Knights and other wealthy men gathered and split into two sides to fight each other."

"To fight each other?" Archer cried. "Maybe I will have to learn how to shoot an arrow!" Archer's eyes— well, one good eye—sparkled at the thought. He did have a shield. Even if *it did* belong to somebody else…

Archer daydreamed of saving an entire military, an entire castle, an entire country.

He would battle King Erik the Plaid's gargantuan, barbarian *army. King Erik the Plaid had heard of Archer's incredible strength from King Elliot the Polka Dot. Archer would defeat* **every single person** *in that* pompous, *plaid-clad man's army.*

And he would do it with only his bare hands!

Once Archer proved he was a hero, King Henry VI & ¾ would gift him the greatest prize in all the land…

And it was there, in those barren fields of Blowendorf, where the brave Sir Archer wedgied the dreaded barbarian, King Erik the Plaid. The barbarian hordes fled to the west, ne'er to return.

Overwhelmed with joyous spirits and gratitude, King Henry VI & ¾ personally served pizza to Sir Archer. Gallant Sir Archer consumed the pie right away.

"No, no. Not a real fight. Tournaments are more for military training. They're like practice battles. And, careful, too many fighting men in one place can lead to a rebellion," Perri corrected, bringing Archer back to reality.

"And knights train in them?" Archer asked.

The two kids looked up. As far as the eye could see—and, in Archer's case, it truly was one eye—there were knights preparing for the tournament.

"Hey!" Archer yelled, "That one is wearing chain mail, too."

"And look!" Perri yelled, "A coat of arms!"

All around them, Perri and Archer saw coats of arms.

GLORIOUS flags proudly presented crowns, horses, lions, snakes, bulls, birds, fish, dragons. Oh, and the colors—the magnificent colors! Rich blues and reds and golds. Because of the intricate designs made of fierce animals and vibrant colors, Perri and Archer couldn't help but feel like each flag or shield was a symbol of **power,** a symbol of **strength.**

"Archer!" Perri said, "Quick, give me the shield."

The kids examined the shield. It had a gold background with a large, gold dragon in the center. Gold swirls that looked like rings of fire encircled the mighty beast. While simple, the shield's design radiated **power** and **strength.**

"Do you think the owner is at this very tournament?" Archer asked, immediately looking about for an incomplete knight.

Just then, a young girl scurried past. The girl moved so quickly that Perri thought she was going to take flight.

She was dressed in a simple light-brown dress. A crisp apron hung from her chest. Perri thought she looked like a maid. The dress and apron were so long that it really did look like she was floating—you couldn't see her feet.

The girl stopped in her tracks and swiveled her head to the side. Her turn was so sharp and precise that it rivaled the arrow that struck Archer.

"You! What are you doing there? Come along—we must **hurry**! We have much to do: apply the calliblephary, brush the butter-teeth, turn the donge. And clean yourself up—you look like a drassock!" the young girl demanded.

Perri and Archer looked at each other with wide eyes.

Perri whispered to Archer: "A calible-what?"

"What is your name?" the young girl asked.

"Uh-uh … Perr-Perri! My name is Perri."

"And I am Elizabeth. I thought we had all of the maids. We must prepare everything before the tilt," Elizabeth said, stomping her foot and motioning her hand for Perri to stand beside her.

"A tilt? What does that mean?" Archer asked.

"A tilt: when two men charge at each other on horseback. The purpose is to unseat the opponent," Elizabeth explained.

"Ohhhh. We call that a joust," Perri said.

"Quite odd. Come along," Elizabeth said, *whisking* Perri away.

And with that, they were gone.

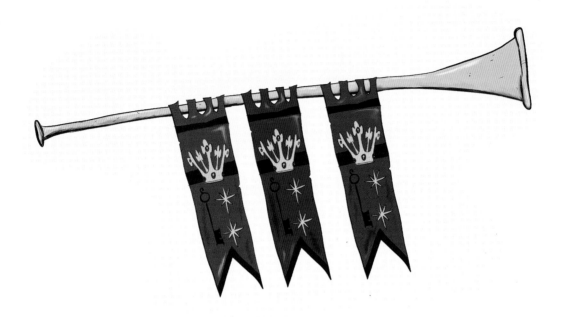

Chapter III: Uh oh, Archer is by himself

With his sister gone to butter a tooth of a lady who needed her cable fixed before her socks dried and the bell rang "ding dong"—at least that's what Archer thought Elizabeth said—Archer continued on his quest to return the coat of arms.

He looked around the field to see if he could match the coat of arms on his shield to any others.

But he stopped in his tracks. All at once, THE SOUND OF 100 HIGH-PITCHED HORNS punctured the hum of tournament preparation.

Archer **gasped.** "I must find Sir Henry. The event is about to begin!" He picked up speed.

Archer **wiggled** his way to the middle of the range. He found a flustered knight—it was Sir Henry. Archer had hoped Sir Henry would not have a shield, but he had one next to his side. "The search for the owner continues," Archer thought.

"Ballard! Where have you been, lad? Quick! Hand me my quiver!" Sir Henry ordered.

"Oh—my name is Archer!" Archer piped up.

"Exactly! *Archery* is now. My quiver, boy!"

Archer spotted a long, thin, leather bag that looked a lot like a mini golf bag. He assumed it was the quiver. He gave Sir Henry a bouquet of arrows and this…quiver? Anxious about his first day on the job, Archer discovered there was a new meaning to an archery quiver. He and Sir Henry's quiver quivered together under the watch of one thousand fans.

Knights released their mighty arrows.

PING!

POW!

WHOOSH!

CRACK!

Sir Henry slowly pulled an arrow from his quiver and loaded it into his bow. He performed this motion with such care and experience that Archer forced himself to open his injured eye. He wanted to take this in.

Sir Henry pulled the bow up and his arrow back. He guided the arrow so it grazed his chin. Archer thought the arrow was so close that he was sure it gave Sir Henry a quick shave.

He released!

And waited.

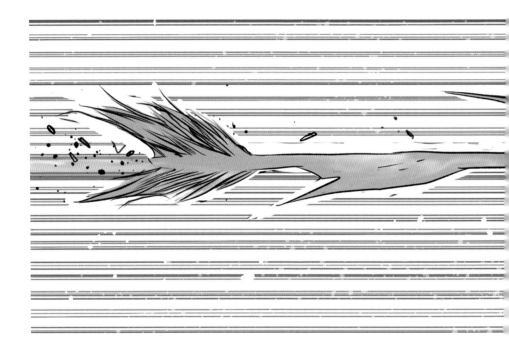

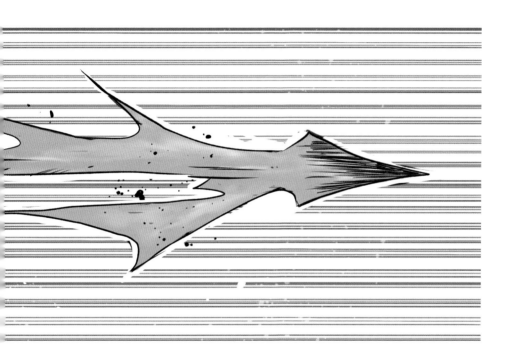

And waited.

The crowd went **wild.**

"Sir, quite a shot!"

"Sir, sir, sir! What is your secret?"

"Sir, please show us your ways!"

Archer beamed from ear to ear—that was his boss!

"Excellent shot, Sir Henry! You really…uh… quivered that right…you really…uh…archered that to the fullest…" Archer offered his compliments, attempting to use the archery terms he just learned… and make up some of his own.

"Gramercy, Ballard!" Sir Henry thanked Archer.

"Oh, I'm sorry! I thought my grammar was correct," Archer said, a bit embarrassed. But, after hearing Sir Henry say "Gramercy" to so many people after they congratulated him, he understood it as "Thank you."

"I'll use that later," Archer thought.

"Halt! You are not Ballard. My page—Ballard! What happened to him?" Sir Henry asked, pushing his face into Archer's and looking him up and down.

"So that's why he called me Ballard," Archer thought. But he did not want to give up this job—his *first* job. He decided to make up a story.

"Well…err…Ballard was wandering around the tournament. And he…uh…got poked in the eye with an arrow…?"

"What a fool," Sir Henry said.

Archer frowned—he didn't *try* to get poked in the eye. Archer didn't have to use too much imagination for this story.

"He saw me and he had heard from *thousands* of my former employees that I was **THE** page of this day and age," Archer said, puffing out his chest.

Sir Henry looked skeptical, but he needed to focus on the coming events. Plus, Archer had come up with such creative compliments for his archery feat.

Sir Henry shrugged, and Archer picked up his supplies, proud of his storytelling. But he did wonder what had happened to Ballard…

Archer knew that lying was bad. Aunt Bubbles had always told them. "Kids," she said, wagging her finger, "being able to tell the truth is a sign of strong character."

"Yes, Aunt Bubbles," Perri and Archer would say in unison.

And they *truly believed* that lying was bad, but Archer didn't want to be revealed as an outsider. He needed to maintain his image as a helpful page from Medieval England. Plus, if people found out that he was an imposter, they might throw him in the dungeon!

The knights, pages, and squires, also known as assistants, made their way back to the striped tents. The assistants attended to their knight's equipment. Archer **seized** on his moment to discover who his shield—and its coat of arms—belonged to.

"Sir Henry, may I ask you about your coat of arms?" Archer asked.

"Why, of course, lad." Sir Henry said, "What would you like to know?"

"Errr …" Archer struggled, "what is it exactly?"

"A coat of arms is a way to identify a knight or a family. Do you see this helmet I'm wearing?"

"Yes, Sir Henry."

"Well, the helmet covers my face during battle. I have a coat of arms—or sometimes we call it a crest—so that my followers can recognize me on the battlefield," Sir Henry explained.

"So you made up the design because your followers were losing you?" Archer asked.

"My ancestors made up the design. It was passed on from generation to generation. Each symbol means something powerful to my family," Sir Henry said.

"What does the bear mean?" Archer asked.

"The bear means **STRENGTH.** But every knight has a different symbol. Sir John, what is on your crest?" Sir Henry asked, addressing one of the many knights in the camp.

"My hawk is for commitment," Sir John revealed.

Like a chorus, the camp of knights explained their crests, each trying to out-do the other.

"I have a lion for **courage!**"

"My family chose a leopard, because we are **WARRIORS!**"

"I am NOBLE, so I wear an eagle."

"I have a cat for liberty!"

"My grandfather was the **FIERCEST** warrior in all the land—we have a boar!"

"See," Sir Henry said, "everyone's crest means something special."

"And what does the color mean? Is your crest red, because you have red hair?" Archer predicted.

"No", Sir Henry roared with a booming and thunderous laugh. "Mine is red, because I am strong. Red symbolizes **STRENGTH.**"

"I'm goofy, so my crest would have a goofy color—like lime green!" Archer proclaimed, thinking of the goofiest color he could. He also considered macaroni-and-cheese yellow or bubblegum pink.

The knights looked confused—curious as to what exactly this "lime green" was.

"Well…regardless of what color you choose, all coats of arms have the same basic design," Sir Henry said, "Bring me my shield."

Archer hoisted Sir Henry's shield onto his lap—all

while thinking of macaroni and cheese after his color choice. In order to give Sir Henry his shield, he put the mystery owner's shield down. He continued with his thoughts on macaroni and cheese.

Taking his shield in his hand, Sir Henry began to trace each part. The other knights gathered around.

Sir Henry explained: "This is the helmet, here on top of the shield. And above the helmet is the crest. This part with the two bears on either side is the supporter."

"Supporter?" Archer asked, "Like who supports you in battle? Like your friends and family?"

"The supporter is the type of knight I am. My ancestors chose two bears to represent **STRENGTH.**" Sir Henry explained, "And a coat of arms has a motto—an important thing you want people to know."

"Ugh, I know what my aunt's motto would be: 'Eat your vegetables,'" Archer said, shuddering in **disgust.** "Sir Henry, do you know who has a crest with a dragon? I am trying to—"

But Archer could not finish his question. The horns **blared** and the horses neighed—the next event was about to begin.

"Hurry, lad! We must not miss it!"

Sir Henry swept Archer up, and they were off! The mystery shield still resting at the camp…

Chapter IV: Meanwhile, at the castle…

Perri and Elizabeth **DASHED** and **DARTED** through the castle. "Wow," Perri thought, "she would make a great outfielder for the softball team—I can hardly keep up."

Perri was in awe of the grand rooms. She especially liked the arches. It seemed like they were the entrance to the sky—they went up and up and up and un'

...e bridges that open up to allow tall boats to pass, she imagined the arches peeling away from the ceiling to reveal millions of stars.

Through a long, thin window, Perri spotted a river flowing far too close to a castle—the **waves** were lapping against the stone wall. "Elizabeth!" Perri shouted, stopping Elizabeth in her path. "A flood is coming!" Perri ducked behind a column that was wider than she and Archer put together.

Elizabeth let out a chuckle…then a giggle…then a big belly laugh.

"You do not know what that is?" Elizabeth asked, trying to hold back even more laughter. "That is woodness!"

"No, no, I know what it is," Perri said, trying to recover and to not embarrass herself. "The castle where I worked before didn't have that…that… woodness," Perri trailed off, searching for the correct word.

"No, no, 'woodness' means **WILD, MAD.** That is a moat," Elizabeth explained.

"A moat? What is it for?"

Elizabeth answered, "A moat is a ditch filled with water."

"Ohhh, we call that a swimming pool. You swim around in it, right? You splash around with friends?" Perri asked.

HORRIFIED, Elizabeth said, "No! No! We do not *play* in the moat! The moat is for keeping enemies out. Thanks to the water, the intruders cannot reach the walls. And when the guards see enemies coming, they raise that over there," Elizabeth said pointing. "That's called a drawbridge."

Perri couldn't help but think that the drawbridge looked like a giant diving board.

"I did not realize you were new to this castle, Perri. I will give you a tour. Once you know the castle, you can move as quickly as I do," Elizabeth offered.

"I don't think I could move as quickly as you even if I was in roller skates," Perri exclaimed.

"Skates?" Elizabeth **quipped** with a shake of her head. "I do not know of what you speak, Perri. Come hither and I will take you on a tour."

As the two girls walked from splendid room to splendid room, Elizabeth described the castle.

"A castle helps kings and people with high status called nobles defend their land. They also use the castle as a home," Elizabeth explained. "Castles have prisons and places to store weapons, too. You know all of this. You worked at a castle. I do not need to explain."

Perri, however, was keen to learn more about the castle, so she replied, "Oh, please, please explain. My old castle was … for-for-for … other … things, " Perri stammered. She hoped her answer wouldn't reveal her status as a newcomer to castles and Medieval England.

"Sometimes, the king uses the castle to host a tournament, such as the one happening outside," Elizabeth continued. Moving, of course, at a **BREAKNECK SPEED.**

"Is there a party after the tournament? After my softball tournaments, we would have a pizza party—err, I mean … At my old castle, there was a big party after the tournaments," Perri said, thankful that she corrected herself. If she and Archer wanted to return the coat of arms, they would have to blend in.

"We have those here, too!" Elizabeth exclaimed, apparently not noticing Perri's pizza remark. "The party is called a feast."

Then, as if on command, the enticing aromas from the feast demanded Perri's attention, capturing her with their sweet and savory scents. She turned her head to see the banquet hall—and what a hall it was!

Rows of wooden tables stretched down the middle of the room with enough seating for all of Perri and Archer's school—and possibly their neighborhood. Large, iron circles with twinkling candles hung from the arched ceiling and illuminated the room. The stone bricks enclosing the hall and keeping the food nice and toasty were stacked as TIGHTLY as Perri's teeth after braces.

After **twirling** under the light fixture and imagining what a pizza party after a softball tournament would look like in *this* room, she caught sight of the food. Her mouth watered.

She saw roasted pig, rabbits smothered in gravy, chicken pastries, and fresh vegetables. She was surprised the vegetables made her excited. "Maybe I would eat vegetables in a room like this," she thought.

But that brief moment of craving vegetables was over when she laid eyes on the apple tart, her favorite dessert.

Seeing how much food there was and wondering who was going to eat it all, Perri asked, "Will the king and queen invite their neighbors?"

"Rulers of castles choose to build in a place surrounded by a lot of empty land," Elizabeth explained, "so they can see attackers in the distance. We do not have close neighbors—the open space is more strategic."

This reason reminded Perri of how she liked to be all by herself in the outfield. It was easier to see

balls flying and players RUNNING,

because the field was not very crowded.

"Come along," Elizabeth whispered, "We have much to do."

As they continued the tour, Elizabeth and Perri passed places to store food and animals, like hounds. Seeing the hounds made Perri think of her own dog, Archie. Yes, it was very confusing having a brother named "Archer" and a dog named "Archie." But, Archer named the dog "Archipelago" after one of his favorite geographical features. But that was *such* a mouthful to yell at the park.

Throughout the castle, Perri noticed the **THICK** stone slabs.

"Elizabeth, why is there so much stone? Don't the kings, queens, and nobles have wood?" Perri asked.

"Why of course they have wood—they have everything your heart desires! But stone is better to protect against enemies, fires, and weather," Elizabeth said.

Always eager to learn new information, Perri stored that in her brain: "It seems like a lot of parts of a castle offer protection," she thought.

An older woman who was dressed a lot like Elizabeth called the girls over. Perri assumed she worked in the kitchen—her face was covered in flour. "We must prepare the feast. We must present ourselves—and present ourselves well."

The cook threw Perri an apron, "Put this on!" she ordered.

Very reluctantly, Perri put on her apron. Aunt Bubbles was always sure not to reinforce gender roles, so she had Perri and Archer both do tasks that some people consider girl tasks or boy tasks.

But, Perri wanted to blend in to Medieval England, so she and Archer could return the shield. She put the apron over her head.

Chapter V: Chapter Five, for those who aren't great with Roman numerals

"Where have you been?!" the cook asked. "We have much bellytimber to ready!"

Perri and Elizabeth followed the cook to the kitchen. The kitchen was very **dark** and smelled of sausages and spices. Even the tools in the kitchen looked like food. The brick walls and loaves of bread were exactly the same color: toasted brown. Some of the bricks on the wall were covered with a white paste. The effect reminded Perri of brownies with cream cheese frosting.

Pots warming *bubbling* stews and sauces hung above a thundering fire. The pots didn't touch the angry fire, thanks to thick strands of rope. With this floating effect, the pots looked like cherries just *begging* to be plucked. Thick planks of wood on the ceiling resembled asparagus on a roasting pan.

"Perri," Elizabeth said, "this is the head cook: Granny Smith."

"Like the type of apple?" Perri thought. "It looked like that **DECADENT** apple tart was made of Granny Smith apples!"

"No time for introductions!" Granny Smith snapped. "Prithee, get to work!"

"Granny Smith?" Elizabeth asked. "Perri is new to the castle, can you show her the kitchen?"

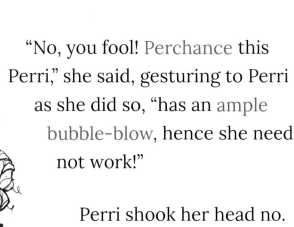

"No, you fool! Perchance this Perri," she said, gesturing to Perri as she did so, "has an ample bubble-blow, hence she need not work!"

Perri shook her head no. She had no idea what bubble-blow meant, but she wondered why Granny Smith would be so angry about bubble gum. She swallowed, just to make sure she didn't have any bubble gum coating the inside her mouth.

"You will assist me," Granny Smith said. "Hand me the **BLOOD.**"

Perri's eyes grew wide.

Then she **gasped.**

A vat—a cauldron, more like it—of **BLOOD** dangled

over the fire. "Oh no, oh no, oh no, oh no! Whose **BLOOD** is this?!" Perri thought. "Please don't let it be Archer's. I knew that if he got into trouble here it would be a different punishment than Aunt Bubbles's, but death?!"

Perri reluctantly handed the pot of **BLOOD** to Granny Smith, closing her eyes and turning her head away from the stinky pot.

"We take **BLOOD** from a pig…"

Perri stopped listening. Phew, the **BLOOD** of a pig! Not the **BLOOD** of her nine-year-old brother.

"We boil the **BLOOD** to make—"

"What do you—"

"No time for questions, lass!" Granny Smith shouted. "We use the black dye for jellies and custards. Next, we prepare that," she said, pointing to a large, grey-black beast in the corner.

A seal.

Perri thought she was going to be sick.

"Why are they eating a cute, slippery, fun-loving seal for dinner? Why not chicken or beef—or tofu!" Perri thought.

"You-You-You are going to," Perri swallowed, "eat that …?"

"Why, of course, girl. Prithee, tell me why you are so dimwitted today!"

Perri stammered.

"Granny Smith!" Elizabeth yelled. "The Lady needs to see Perri." Elizabeth whisked Perri away. For once, Perri was so happy about Elizabeth's speed. Perri was thankful that Elizabeth helped her—she didn't know if she could stomach **BLOOD** and seals in the same day.

"Follow me," Elizabeth said. "We're off to the tournament!" Perri—slightly **nauseous**—followed.

Chapter VI: Who is this checkered chap?

Archer followed the other knights around the tournament. Given his boss's archery success, he considered Sir Henry the star of the day.

He walked through the tournament easier than before. He felt so light, in fact, that Archer was sure he was missing something.

He thought.

And thought.

But nothing.

He, of course, was missing the shield. But, he was sure he had everything he came with, so he carried on.

He came across a fellow in a funny outfit. He wore a checkered coat with tights. Both were made up of many different colors. He **jingled** and **jangled,** *flipped* and *flopped*. Bells adorned his head, shoulders, knees, and toes. Archer thought his long, pointed shoes would be perfect for tripping—and his assumption was correct!

Oomph!

Archer stumbled to the ground.

The checkered man **skipped** over to him.

"Sir, I say, you do not look so well. Is it perhaps because you fell? Watch your step, my little lad. Fall again and you will feel so sad," the man said in a **singsong** voice.

"Huh?" Archer asked, "I'm okay...who are you?"

"Why I am the jester. I bring joy to the royals with song and gesture. I ask a riddle and play the fiddle. My job is to make the king laugh, and, oh, if I do not succeed, I will face his wrath!"

"So, you tell a joke to avoid a poke, and dance, dance, dance to avoid the lance?" Archer asked, mimicking his new friend.

"Exactly! Sir, look over there!" the jester directed, pointing his finger in the direction of the castle.

Archer turned around and looked in that direction. "I don't see anything," Archer said.

"Ha! I fooled you—I made you look! Learn, my friend—that is the oldest trick in the book!"

"Ooo! Ooo! I have one," Archer said, eager to impress his tricky, rhythmic friend with a joke of his own.

83

"My dear lad, I do not comprehend. Though I am so glad that poor joke has come to an end. To be a good jester, you mustn't let a joke fester. You must be quick as a fox, and—please, my dear boy—no more 'Knock knocks.'"

The sheep was equally as delighted the joke had come to an end.

Archer still thought it was funny, so he unleashed a **roar of laughter.**

Archer returned to the area where knights fought. It was called the list. A large, flat field of dirt was in the center of rows and rows of seating. The area reminded Archer of a football field, because of people sitting up high to watch the event.

A long fence-like barrier split the field in two. A knight and his horse stood at either end of the field, readying themselves to charge towards one another.

The crowd was in an **uproar**—the event was

about to begin. But as Archer approached, he found a **nervous** knight.

The knight mumbled to himself, "Oh, Cedric, how could you do this, you fool? What will father think? What will grandfather think? What would great-grandfather think?! I have disgraced my family and my people. Oh, what a fool I am. Oh, what a fool..."

Archer interjected, "Excuse me, Sir."

Archer interrupted the knight from his thoughts. "My name is Archer. I'm Sir Henry's page. How may I help you? What's happened?" Archer asked.

"I do not know where my shield is. And it has my coat of arms on it. It represents everything my family stands for. I cannot joust without it … Sir Cedric," the knight said, extending his hand to shake Archer's. Shield or not, he *did* have to maintain his knightly honor.

"How did you misplace it?"

"I am so fond of maps, I thought I might do a bit of exploring before my event. I did not want to be weighed down with my shield, so I rested it over there," Sir Cedric explained, pointing to a spot without a shield.

"You like maps!?" Archer asked.

"Why of course, young page. As contradictory as it may sound, I get lost in them, in their beauty. I—"

Archer interrupted Sir Cedric, "Am in awe of the way they explain the world around you?'

"Precisely!"

Archer was getting so excited about this courageous cartographer! Aunt Bubbles taught him the word "cartographer." She said it meant a person who makes maps. Suddenly, he remembered the shield.

"Sir Cedric," Archer started, "does your shield have a dragon on it?"

"Why, yes. Yes it does. Have you seen it? It is a beautiful gold color with gold swirls that wind and wind around the dragon," said Sir Cedric, getting lost in the memory of his beloved accessory.

The shield fit the description. Archer reached behind him for the shield, ready to present it to Sir Cedric. **WOW!** What an adventure! What a first day of work! What a—

Wait, what?

Where was the shield?

"I've been carrying that thing all day—it weighs a billion-kajillion pounds!" Archer thought. "Did I lose it? Did that jester take it?! I knew I didn't trust him, not liking my 'Knock knocks' and all..."

The camp! Archer had left the mystery shield at the camp! It happened before he met the jester... "So, I guess he wasn't such a bad guy," Archer thought.

"Sir Cedric, can you hold on for, like, one minute?" Archer asked, pointing his finger to indicate one minute.

Archer sprinted back to the knights's warm-up area. "Please, oh please, let the shield be there. If I find it, I promise I'll be so, so, so nice to Aunt Bubbles. I'll eat broccoli—and even cauliflower!" Archer said.

He saw knights and pages and squires and horses

and other coats of arms, but not the one he wanted.

And then he halted. He saw a boy just like him. He had curly hair like Archer. He was the same size as Archer. He thought he was looking in a mirror.

"Ballard?" Archer asked.

The young boy looked up from his turkey leg. He was sitting on the ground gnawing the leg until the bones were so small you could make toothpicks.

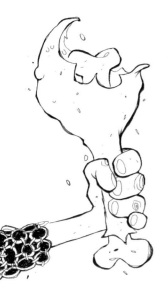

"Mmhmmm," Ballard confirmed, chewing on the crisp skin.

"Umm…what are you doing?" Archer asked.

"Eat—eating!" Ballard said, between bites.

Archer did not want to give up his job. "Well then, carry on!"

Archer continued searching for the shield. He thought Ballard would understand. They were basically twins, after all. He was glad his eye was feeling better—he certainly needed both.

Success!

There, resting on the ground, was the shield—fully intact. Archer breathed a huge sigh of relief.

He dashed back to Sir Cedric. He moved a bit more slowly, given that he was carrying the shield. But Archer had never been happier to carry this thing—even if it did weigh as much as ten elephants.

Archer proudly presented the shield to Sir Cedric.

"Oh! My savior! Gramercy! Gramercy! Where did you find it?" Sir Cedric asked.

"Oh … uh … just over there," Archer said **nervously,** pointing to a random spot he hoped Sir Cedric wouldn't want to investigate.

"You are the finest page in all the land!" Sir Cedric proclaimed.

"WOW," Archer thought, "I didn't just get 'Employee of the Month' on my first job—I got 'Employee of the Land'!"

The horns announced the joust was about to begin.

"Gramercy, page! I must compete!" Sir Cedric announced, steadying himself for this much-anticipated event.

"Good luck, my dear Sir Cedric! Now it's time for my last trick. We want your mind free and without block. May I suggest a calming 'Knock knock'?" Archer asked in a **singsong** voice.

"Who's there?" Sir Cedric asked.

"See! You get it! We're soulmates!" Archer declared, basing his verdict off of their love of maps and appreciation for a good "Knock knock" joke.

Sir Cedric was off to challenge a knight. Strapped with his shield, he was ready to fight!

Chapter VII: Cedric and Shield: Together at last

Perri took her place beside the other maids to watch the competition. She couldn't believe her eyes—the **SPECTACLE** of it all! The excitement of the tournament masked Perri's upset stomach, and the **BLOOD** and the seal seemed like a distant memory.

Perri looked at the world around her—and what a **spectacular** world it was. She breathed in the smell and committed the scene to memory. She was thinking about how pleasant the adventure was when she let out a shriek.

EEEEEEEPPPPPPPPPPPPPPPPPP!

"Archer! He is going to joust!" Perri *YELLED.*

Standing before her eyes, preparing to face a vicious opponent, was a knight on a horse carrying the shield from Lost & Found!

The Mustachioed Monster could smell the sweet smell of his impending victory. The crowd could smell something less sweet coming from his horse.

His opponent, Sir Cedric—*not* Archer—underdog but unafraid, grasped firmly the shield so recently returned to him. His family's coat of arms gave him extra courage.

A booming brong broke Perri and Archer's embrace.

BRONG

"I'm glad your only—

BRONG

"injury is your adorable ear with the chunk missing. And, I guess, your eye. The **BRONGS** are coming. It's time to go return home," Perri said.

BRONG

"I see the *bubbles* in the distance. Look—it looks like they are moving that speedy maid who *whisked* you away," Archer said.

"So that explains her speed …" Perri said.

The final **BRONGS** reverberated off the thick, stone slabs of the castle. Perri and Archer were traveling forward in time, forward to Lost & Found.

Chapter VIII: Farewell, Medieval England

The kids landed with a **thud.**

"Wh-wh-wh-where are we?" Archer asked, rubbing his head.

Stray bubbles floated back into the grandmother clock.

CLAP!

The World Book **SLAPPED** shut.

"Ahhhhh!" Perri screamed. "Oh, it's just *The World Book*. The final piece in this time-traveling puzzle."

Archer wriggled himself free of the chain mail with a great sigh of relief.

They trekked through the Bucolic Land of Lost Buttons. Over the Bumpy Bridge of Broken China and under the Voluminous Valley of Vintage Vanities.

They came upon Aunt Bubbles.

"Good eve, Aunt Bubbles. We certainly haven't been causing troubles. I've just been playing with Perri, my comrade. We're so happy to see you—oh, we're so glad!" Archer exclaimed.

Perri and Archer's aunt looked confused.

"Pray, tell, what is our meal? I hope not seal. I long for macaroni and cheese—oh, please Aunt Bubbles, please?!"

"Arch," Aunt Bubbles asked, "why all the rhyming?"

"I've decided to be the family jester," Archer announced proudly.

Aunt Bubbles didn't act the least bit surprised. It was the kind of thing Archer would do.

After dinner—a dinner that, thanks to Archer's urging, was macaroni and cheese—Perri thought of an idea. "We should make a family crest."

"What a great idea!" Archer said.

Perri and Archer explained everything they had learned about crests—careful not to reveal *how* they learned the information.

Together, the family thought of ideas.

"I think we should make it white—for peace," Perri offered.

"Yeah! And a tortoise, because it lives a long time— that way it can see a lot of history," Archer chimed in.

Perri asked, "What's the family motto?"

The family thought.

And thought.

I know, Aunt Bubbles said …

THE END

Epilogue
(that's the bit after the story)

Perri here. We wanted to learn more about where we were. We also thought you might want to, too. The medieval period is also called the Middle Ages. This period lasted a very long time: the 400's through the 1400's. That means about a thousand years. People who study the period divide it into three sections: early Middle Ages, High Middle Ages, and late Middle Ages. There were major advances in a bunch of fields: art, culture, society, trade, politics, and language.

The High Middle Ages interested us most. The population peaked during the High Middle Ages. Towns grew, too. Many of the townspeople achieved wealth and influence. This changed the traditional image of society which was made up of lords, clergy—leaders in the church—and peasants. With new prosperity, people could focus on new ideas and activities. The towns were centers of production. People made stuff: ceramics, cloth, glass, and leather goods.

Archer here. Remember when Perri thought I was about to fight the biggest, meanest, largest-mustached knight I had ever seen? Of course you do, that's the whole point of the story. Well, they were about to do something called jousting.

Jousting happened during tournaments. It could also happen all over different parts of a countryside. Royal rulers didn't love tournaments. They thought they were bloody and wasteful. So, the people in charge made it a rule that you could only have a tournament with their permission.

The speedy maid, Elizabeth, called jousting "tilting." She wasn't just saying a random word—and it also turns out that those weird words she said *were* terms from the medieval period. Tilting is one form of jousting. Tilting was when two knights on horseback charged at each other. It happened on a list, and rails kept the horses apart. The goal of tilting was to knock your opponent off his horse.

Now it's both of us. Remember how we told you to pay attention to the purple words? Well, now we are going to tell you why. It's because those words are difficult words that either we learned or we used or the writer of this book put in to make the book better. Also, some of these words have multiple meanings. So we defined them in terms of how they are used in this book.

ample: plentiful; a lot

anon: later on

archery: the sport of shooting a bow and arrow; what Sir Archer is awesome at

assumption: belief without proof

barbarian: violent person; King Erik the Plaid

bellytimber: food

bubble-blow: a lady's wallet

bucolic: pleasant; idyllic

butter-teeth: what you use to eat bellytimber

calliblephary: eye makeup; what Aunt Bubbles uses *way* too much of

contradictory: doesn't match; goes against something

conundrum: a confusing situation

decadent: rich (in terms of food: really, *really* flavorful)

dimwitted: stupid; easily confused by conundrums

donge: mattress

drassock: a woman who isn't tidy; Perri (sometimes)

effervescent: high-spirited; joyous; bubbly; Aunt Bubbles

enticing: tempting; making you want something; the smells from an apple tart

fester: rot; get bad

gargantuan: enormous; like so big you couldn't believe it

gnawing: like nibbling

hither: here; like, "Come here."

hordes: a bunch of people

illuminated: lit up

impending: about to happen

imposter: someone who pretends to be something

keen: eager

lance: pointy, sword-like thing

mimicking: Mimicking (Hint: copying or imitating)

mischievous: naughty or troublesome; Archie…and, sometimes, Archer

morrow: the not-so-distant future

mutton: food…that is sheep

perchance: perhaps

pompous: the person thinks they are the greatest thing since sliced bread; self-important

pop-beak: fictional snack made of pigeon beaks; somehow, even though it is fictional, Archer's favorite snack

prithee: please; what Aunt Bubbles always tells us to say

quipped: remark in a funny or witty (clever) way

radiated: extend; go outward

reverberated: vibrated; pulsed

savory: not sweet; the flavor that mutton is

skeptical: doubtful; Aunt Bubbles when we tell her we've finished all of our homework

vanities: tables where you would put on calliblephary

verdict: a decision

vintage: antique; Aunt Bubbles

voluminous: immense; kind of like "ample"

wrath: anger, like, *terrible* anger

Written by
Madeline King

Illustrated by
Scott Brown

Directed by Tom Evans
Designed by Melanie Bender
Illustration colored by Francis Paola Lea
Cover and additional illustration by Dave Shepherd
Proofread by Nathalie Strassheim

With special thanks to:

Robbin Brosterman and Lucie Luddington of The Bright Agency,
Evie Beckett, Anne Fritzinger, Grace Guibert, Linda King, Mohan Kulik,
the Perry family, Rubric Sane, Rebecca Sullivan, and Lillian Tanner.
Oh, and Aunt Bubbles.

World Book, Inc.
180 North LaSalle Street, Suite 900
Chicago, Illinois 60601
USA

For information about other "Lost & Found" titles, as well as other World Book
print and digital publications, please go to www.worldbook.com.

For information about other World Book publications, call 1-800-WORLDBK (967-5325).

For information about sales to schools and libraries,
call 1-800-975-3250 (United States) or 1-800-837-5365 (Canada).

Library of Congress Cataloging-in-Publication Data for this volume has been applied for.

Lost & Found
ISBN: 978-0-7166-2807-1 (set, hc.)

Coat of Arms Conundrum
Perri and Archer's (mis)adventure in Medieval England
ISBN: 978-0-7166-2808-8 (hc.)

Also available as:
ISBN: 978-0-7166-2814-9 (e-book)

Printed in China by RR Donnelley, Guangdong Province
1st printing July 2019